Don't Wake Up the Bear!

by **Marjorie Dennis Murray**
Illustrated by **Patricia Wittmann**

Marshall Cavendish ☾ New York

Marshall Cavendish, 99 White Plains Road,
Tarrytown, NY 10591
www.marshallcavendish.com

Library of Congress Cataloging-in-Publication Data
Murray, Marjorie Dennis.
Don't wake up the bear! / by Marjorie Dennis Murray ;
illustrations by Patricia Wittmann.
p. cm.
Summary: On a cold, snowy evening several animals
snuggle up to a hibernating bear in order to keep warm.
ISBN 0-7614-5107-2
[1. Bears--Fiction. 2. Animals--Fiction. 3. Hibernation--
Fiction.] I.
Wittmann, Patricia, ill. II. Title.
PZ7.M9635 Do 2003   [E]--dc21   2002006813

The text of this book is set in 14 point Berling.
The illustrations are rendered in watercolor.
Printed in China
First edition
6 5 4 3 2 1

To my brother, James A. Putnam, fellow writer and theoretical physicist, who can calculate the amount of energy needed to wake up a bear

—M.D.M.

For Sophie, a girl who loves stories

—P.W.

One cold winter's eve
a bear lay asleep in his cave.
The bear was big.
The bear was soft.
The bear was warm.

In the woods a silver hare stopped to rest. She noticed the bear.

"My ears are so . . . cold," said the hare. "I wish I could snuggle up with that big, soft, warm bear."

And since her ears were so cold, and the bear was fast asleep, she did.

A badger came by, his muzzle white with snow. He saw the hare snuggled against the bear.

"My nose is so . . . cold," said the badger. "I wish I could snuggle up with that big, soft, warm bear."

"*You may come in,*" whispered the hare. *"But don't wake up the bear!"*

And since the badger's nose was so cold, and the bear was fast asleep, he did.

Along came a fox. He saw the badger and the hare snuggled against the bear.

"My legs are so . . . cold," said the fox. "I wish I could snuggle up with that big, soft, warm bear."

"You may come in," whispered the hare. *"But don't wake up the bear!"*

And since the fox's legs were so cold, and the bear was fast asleep, he did.

A squirrel scampered out of his tree. He saw the fox and the badger
and the hare snuggled against the bear.

"My toes are so . . . cold," said the squirrel. "I wish I could snuggle up
with that big, soft, warm bear."

"*You may come in,*" whispered the hare. "*But don't wake up the bear!*"
And since the squirrel's toes were so cold, and the bear was fast
asleep, he did.

A little mouse skirted by,
slipping on the ice. She saw the
squirrel and the fox and the
badger and the hare snuggled
against the bear.

"My tail is so . . . cold," sniffed
the mouse. "I wish I could
snuggle up with that big, soft,
warm bear."

"*You may come in,*" whispered
the hare. And then she said . . .
"*But don't wake up the bear!*"

And since the bear's ear looked so soft,
and the bear was fast asleep, she did.

In the woods, snowflakes drifted down, softly, softly down,
and everything was quiet . . .

. . .until . . . from deep within
the darkness and the comfy,
cozy softness, there came a little
sniffle . . . and the mouse awoke
with a twitchy little nose . . . and
a great BIG sniffle.

"HUSH!" whispered the hare.
And then she said, *"Don't wake
up the bear!"*

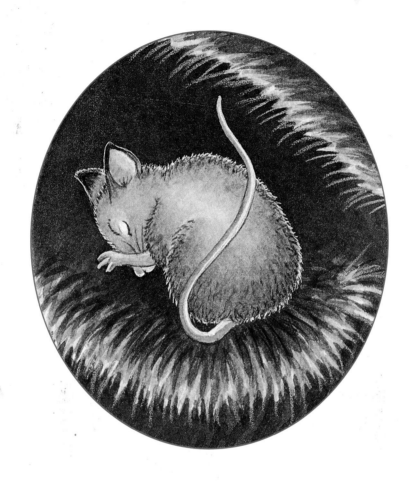

But the mouse didn't hear. She was much too busy scrinching her nose and sniffling. She sniffed and she sniffled and she sniffled and she sniffed.

"HUSH!" said the squirrel and the fox and the badger and the hare. And then they said, *"Don't wake up the bear!"*

From the middle of the bear there came a rumble and a grumble.

"I—I—I'm sorry," said the mouse, "but I—I have a c-c-cold and I—I ha-have to . . .

Ah-CHOOOOO!",

and she sneezed right in the
bear's ear!
   The bear shuddered . . .
the bear trembled . . . the bear
rumbled . . . the bear grumbled
. . . and the bear . . .

Woke up!

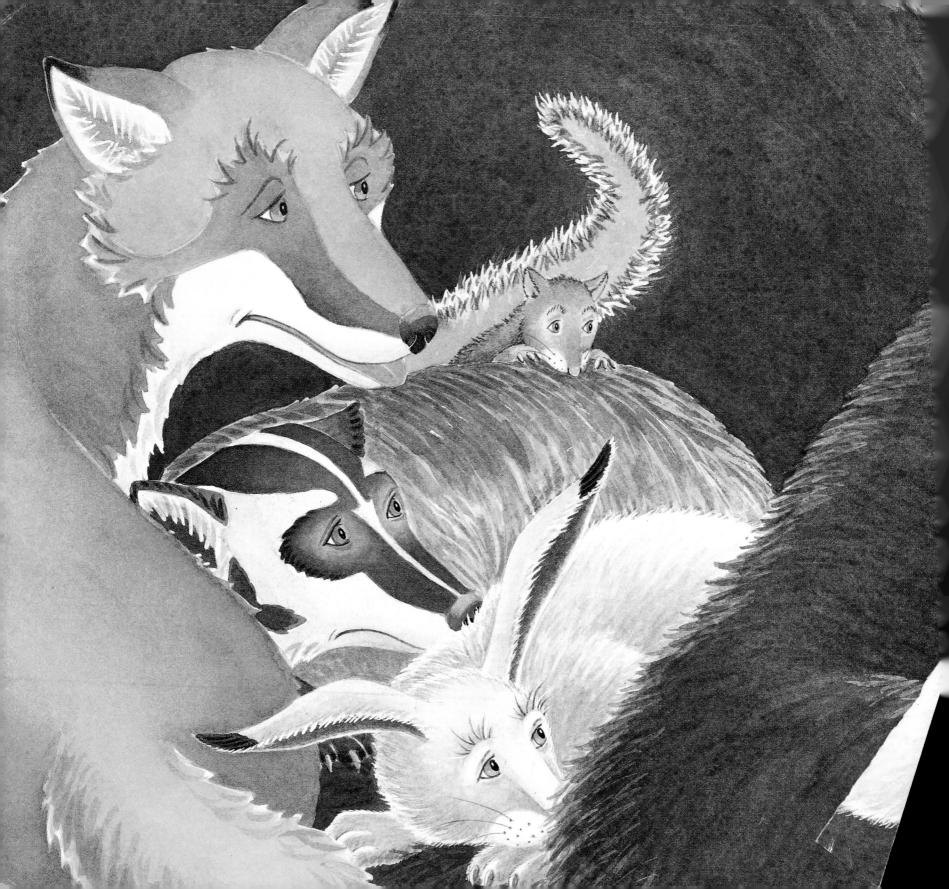

And he was very hungry!

He looked around.

He saw the mouse.

He saw the squirrel.

He saw the fox.

He saw the badger.

He saw the hare.

Then he opened wide

his **huge Bear Mouth...**

. . . and **growled** the **loudest growl** ever heard from a bear.

GRRRTOOOOOOOOOOOOWLL!!!

The mouse froze with terror.

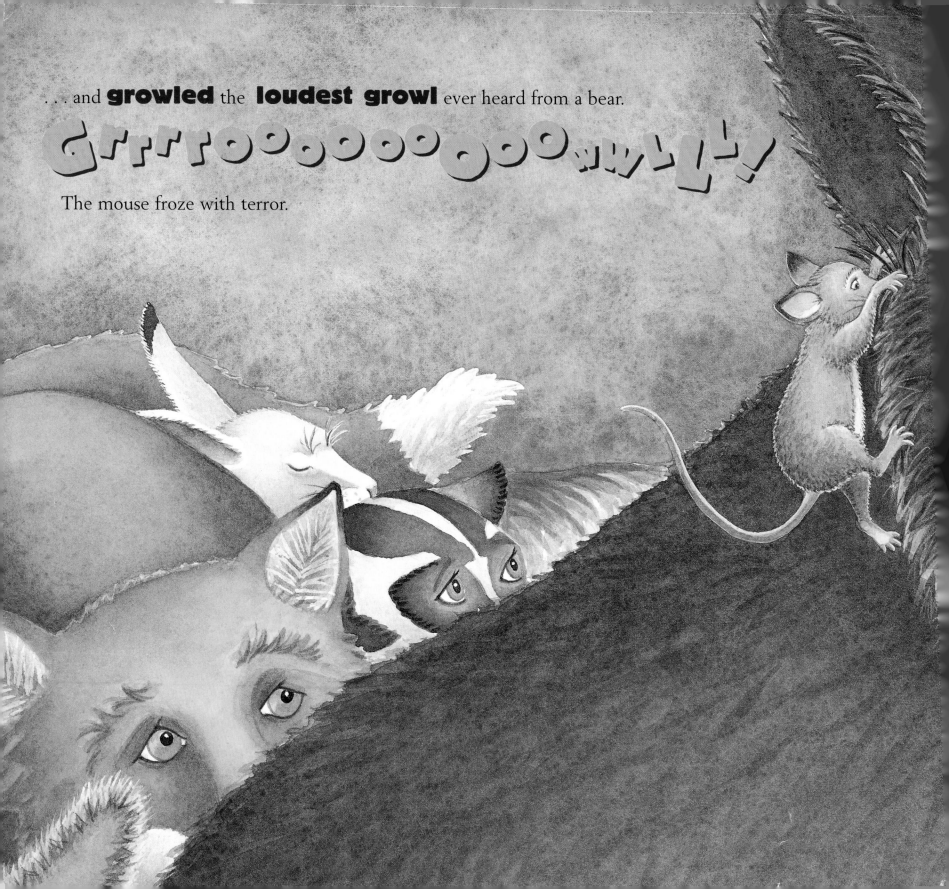

"RUN, LITTLE MOUSE!"

shouted the squirrel and the fox and the badger and the hare.

"He's HUNGRY!"

This time the little mouse listened, for she couldn't help but hear.

And away they all ran—the mouse, the squirrel, the fox, the badger, and the hare, slipping and sliding through the woods as fast as they could go.

And the bear? He yawned a

big . . . soft . . . warm,

bear yawn,

stumbled to his feet, and

trudged off through the snow. . .

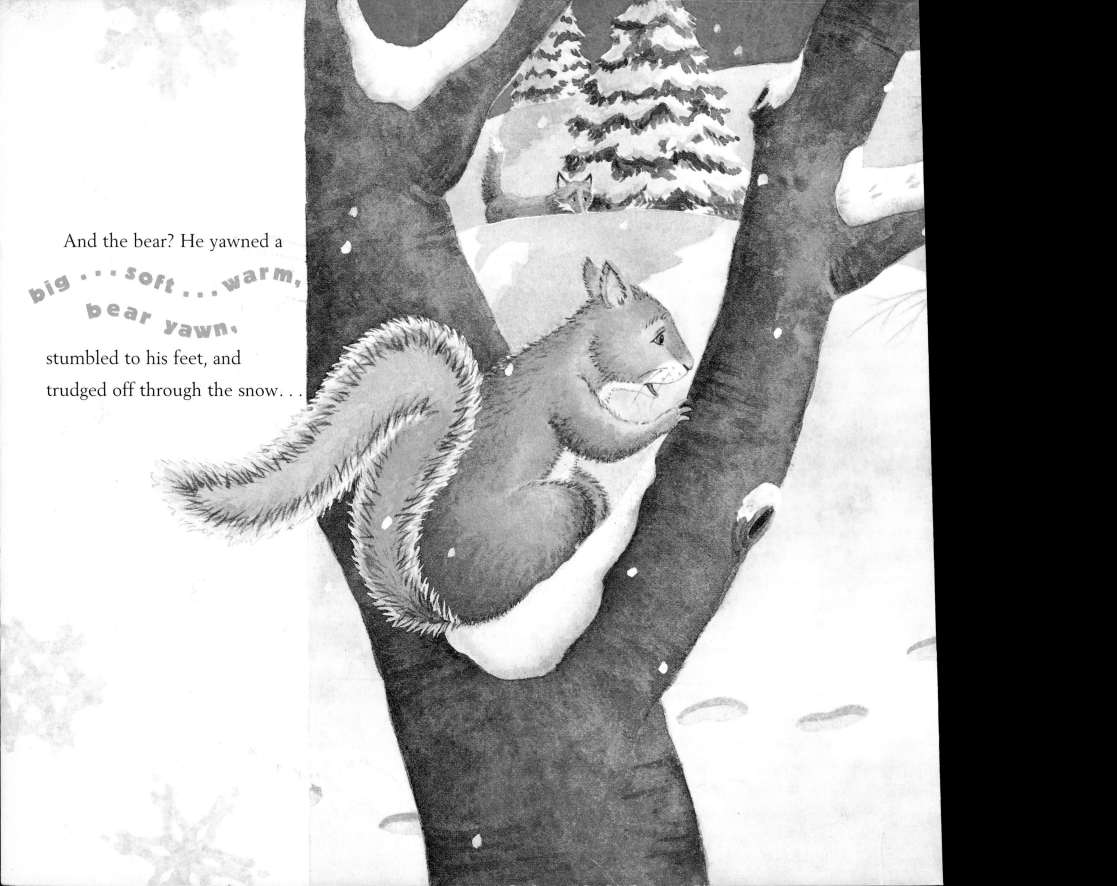

. . . to find something to eat.